COUNTRIES IN THE NEWS
FRANCE

Kieran Walsh

Rourke
Publishing LLC
Vero Beach, Florida 32964

www.rourkepublishing.com

The country's flag is correct at the time of going to press.

PHOTO CREDITS: ©Pascal Le Segretain/Getty Images pg 13; ©Doug Pensinger/Getty Images pg 15; ©Patrick Kovarik/AFP/Getty Images pg 18; ©Peter Langer Associated Media Group Title, pg 7; ©DigitalVision pg 10; ©ArtToday, Inc. Cover, pgs 4, 6 ©Craig Young pgs 8, 9; ©Helen Lee pg 19; ©Reto Morgenthaler pg 12 ©Stella Reese pg 17; ©Athewma pg 11

Title page: *One of the world's most famous museums, the Louvre, is in Paris.*

Editor: Frank Sloan

Cover and interior design by Nicola Stratford

Library of Congress Cataloging-in-Publication Data

Walsh, Kieran.
  France / Kieran Walsh.
      p. cm. — (Countries in the news II)
  Includes bibliographical references and index.
  ISBN 1-59515-172-9 (hardcover)
  1. France--Juvenile literature. I. Title. II. Series: Walsh, Kieran. Countries in the news II.
  DC33.W35 2004
  944—dc22

                                        2004009682

Printed in the USA

CG/CG

TABLE OF CONTENTS

Welcome to France 4

The People..8

Life in France 12

School and Sports 14

Food and Holidays..16

The Future 18

Fast Facts..20

The Channel Tunnel 21

Glossary 22

Further Reading..23

Websites to Visit..23

Index..24

WELCOME TO
FRANCE

France is one of the largest countries in Europe. It is slightly smaller than the state of Texas.

France has a varied landscape that includes **fertile** plains and a number of mountain ranges.

A well-known monument in Paris, the Arch of Triumph

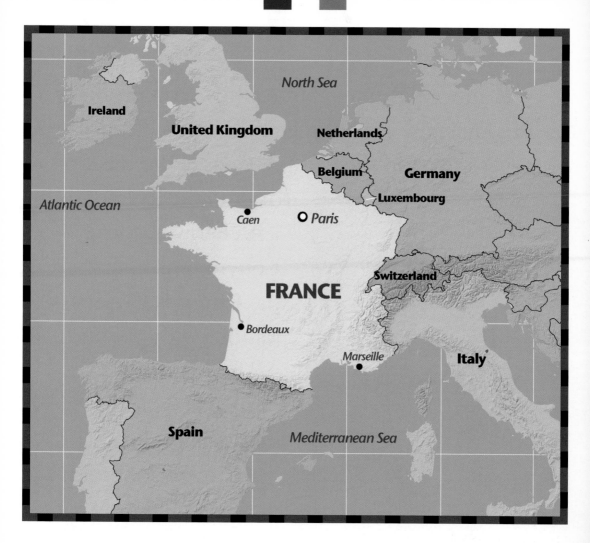

The Pyrenees, for instance, are located in the southwest along the border with Spain. The Alps, meanwhile, run along France's eastern border with Italy and Switzerland.

France also has a number of long rivers, including the Loire and the Seine.

France has many large cities. You probably already know something about Paris, France's largest city and the capital. Paris is the location of **landmarks** like the Eiffel Tower, the Louvre museum, and the Champs Elysées, a famous wide avenue.

The weather in France is typically mild. Rainfall is light, and temperatures in the summer are usually in the high 70s° F (21° C).

One of the world's best known sights, the Eiffel Tower

Many artists like to sketch subjects by the banks of the Seine River.

THE PEOPLE

The majority of the people who live in France were born there. However, some of the population are German, Italian, and Portuguese. France is also seeing an increase in the number of **immigrants** from North Africa.

Most of the French are Roman Catholic, but the Jewish population in France is the second highest in Europe. The Muslim population of France numbers between 3 and 5 million.

Sidewalk cafés are popular in many French cities.

Towering above the city of Paris is the famous church of Sacre Coeur.

France has a superb national health care system. Because of this, the life expectancy for most people is 79 years.

It is estimated that 75 percent of the French population live and work in big cities like Paris.

The high-speed French TGV train crosses a bridge.

The old and new: the Louvre museum at the left and the recently built pyramid in the court, taken at night

Many French who live in the countryside work as farmers.

LIFE IN FRANCE

Life in France is very similar to daily life in the United States. One big exception is that every year, French workers are given five weeks of paid vacation. Most people take this time off during July and August and travel to one of France's many resort towns.

A view of sunny southern France's Riviera, near the city of Nice

It snows only rarely in Paris!

Most of these places, including Saint-Tropez, Nice, and Cannes, are located along the Mediterranean Sea. This part of France is known as the French Riviera. Some families even own vacation homes in these parts of the country.

SCHOOL AND SPORTS

French children attend public elementary school from the ages of 6 to 11. After this, they attend a four-year school not unlike a junior high. At the age of 15, students enter a **lycée**, a kind of school **maintained** by the government. The lycée prepares students either for joining the French workforce or for further study at one of the country's 75 universities.

Soccer is the most popular sport in France, although people also enjoy tennis and rugby. The world-famous Tour de France bicycle race is held every summer.

Riders in the Tour de France cross the Champs Elysées.

The literacy rate in France is 99%.

FOOD AND HOLIDAYS

Perhaps the food most readily associated with France is **fromage**, or cheese. A large variety of cheeses come from France, including Roquefort, Camembert, and Brie.

Other French favorites include **croissants**, a buttery pastry, and **soufflés**, a dish made from eggs, cream, and a third ingredient that can be anything from ham or broccoli to chocolate.

Although the French observe many of the same holidays that we do in America, they also celebrate holidays that are not so familiar. Every July 14, for example, is **Bastille** Day. This is a holiday that marks the storming of a prison called the Bastille in 1789. This event marked the end of France as a monarchy and its start as a republic.

A typical French breakfast consists of milky coffee and a pastry.

THE FUTURE

In 2002 and 2003, relations between France and the United States were strained. More often than not, though, France has been an **ally** of the United States.

French president Jacques Chirac greets schoolchildren.

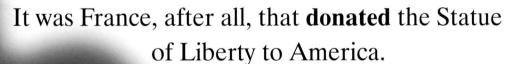

It was France, after all, that **donated** the Statue of Liberty to America. Despite recent hardships, including an unusual heat wave that resulted in the deaths of several thousand people, France will likely remain an important world power for years to come.

New York's landmark Statue of Liberty was a gift from France in 1886.

FAST FACTS

Area: 211,208 square miles (546,986 sq km)

Borders: France shares borders with the countries of Belgium, Luxembourg, Germany, Switzerland, Italy, and Spain, along with the principalities of Andorra and Monaco. France also touches the English Channel, the Atlantic Ocean, the Bay of Biscay, and the Mediterranean Sea

Population: 60,180,529
Monetary Unit: The euro

Largest Cities: Paris, Nice, Cannes
Government: Republic

Religions: Roman Catholic, Protestant, Muslim, Jewish
Crops: Wheat, cereal, sugar, potatoes, beef

Natural Resources: Coal, iron ore, bauxite, timber, fish
Major Industries: Automobiles, aircraft, chemicals, electronics, tourism

THE CHANNEL TUNNEL

One of the most **ambitious** engineering projects of recent years was the building of the Channel Tunnel, a railroad connecting France and the United Kingdom.

Sometimes called the "Chunnel," the Channel Tunnel includes three tunnels, each 31 miles (50 km) long. These tunnels are located roughly 150 feet (46 m) below the English Channel, the body of water between England and France.

Construction of the Chunnel took place between 1986 and 1994. The Chunnel allows people to travel between the cities of London and Paris in only a matter of hours.

GLOSSARY

ally (AL EYE) — a friend of

ambitious (am BISH us) — daring, bold

Bastille (bah STEEL) — a noted prison in Paris

croissants (KWA sahntz) — small, buttery pastries

donated (doh NAYT ed) — gave to

fertile (FURT ill) — good for growing

fromage (FRO MAHJ) — the French word for cheese

immigrants (IM uh grantz) — people who move from one country to another

landmarks (LAND MARKZ) — important places or things

lycée (LIH SAY) — a type of French school

maintained (MAYN taynd) — run by

soufflés (SOO FLAYZ) — cooked dishes of eggs, cream, and other ingredients

FURTHER READING

Find out more about France with these helpful books:

- Bramwell, Martyn. *The World in Maps: Europe.* Lerner Publications, 2000
- Chandler, Virginia. *The Changing Face of France.* Raintree/Steck Vaughn, 2002
- Corona, Laurel. *France (Modern Nations of the World).* Lucent Books, 2002
- Nardo, Don. *Enchantment of the World: France.* Children's Press, 2000
- Park, Ted. *Taking Your Camera to France.* Steadwell Books, 2000
- Sommers, Michael A. *France: A Primary Source Cultural Guide.* Rosen/PowerKids, 2004

WEBSITES TO VISIT

- www.info-france-usa.org/
  Embassy of France in the United States
- www.gofrance.about.com/
  About.com – France for Visitors
- www.infoplease.com/ipa/A0107517.html
  Infoplease – France

INDEX

Alps   5

Bastille Day   16

Champs Elysées   6

Channel Tunnel   21

croissants   16

Eiffel Tower   6

French Riviera   13

fromage   16

Loire   5

Louvre (museum)   6

lycée   14

Nice   13

Paris   6, 10, 21

Pyrenees   5

Saint-Tropez   13

Seine   5

soufflés   16

Statue of Liberty   19

Tour de France   14

About the Author

Kieran Walsh is a writer of children's nonfiction books, primarily on historical and social studies topics. Walsh has been involved in the children's book field as editor, proofreader, and illustrator as well as author.